# Super God

# Super God

## Kristina Eklund

# Super God

Published by
Lighthouse Christian Publishing
SAN 257-4330
5531 Dufferin Drive
Savage, Minnesota, 55378
United States of America

www.lighthousechristianpublishing.com

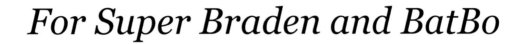

*For Super Braden and BatBo*

*There are super heroes that are big and superheroes that are small...but have you ever wondered, who is the greatest super hero of all???*

Is he the one with Super built right in his name?
That's flying and speed brought him great fame.

Kristina Eklund

The one with icy cold breath and x -ray vision,
Who keeps Metropolis safe with expert precision?

By day he's a businessman, at night he fights crime,
He serves and protects Gotham all of the time.

Or is it the woman in the invisible jet,
The Amazon princess and crime solving vet?

Or could it be a team of acrobatic turtles
Who guard the sewer from all of the villainous hurdles?

Adolescent mutants that are named after artists,
And work together with the power they harness.

No, the greatest of all doesn't wear a cape,
He doesn't dress like a bat, turtle or ape.

He doesn't have an alter ego or secret identity.
He's three heroes in one and that is His entity.

He isn't limited by one power, vehicle or gadget.
He doesn't fight crime in once city or planet.

Kristina Eklund

His powers are
limitless because
he is the maker
of all!
And He is here for
you always,
whenever you call!!

To summon His help, you don't need a signal. You needn't be in church or sing from a hymnal.

All you need is to believe in Him and all that he can do! Our God is the greatest hero that can ever help you!

Nothing can stop our Super God,
His strength is far reaching without any flaw.

He can't be defeated by weapons or even kryptonite.
No villain stands a chance against God in a fight!

So, when you are in trouble and are in need of saving,
Call out to Super God, the hero most amazing!!

Made in the USA
San Bernardino, CA
23 April 2018